S0-AYI-483

To:
Mr. Davis
Dare to Dream!

Granny McFanny

Lewis Kimberly

Illustrations by Jorge Betancourt Polanco

Stephens Press ∗ Las Vegas, Nevada

Copyright 2008 Stephens Press, LLC
Text: Lewis Kimberly
Illustrations: Jorge Betancourt Polanco
All Rights Reserved

No portion of this book may be reproduced in any form or by any
means without permission in writing from the publisher, except
for the inclusion of brief quotations in a review.

Layout: Sue Campbell

Library of Congress Cataloging in Publication Data

Kimberly, Lewis.
   Granny McFanny / Lewis Kimberly ; illustrated by Jorge Betancourt Polanco.
32 p. : ill. ; 30 cm.
   ISBN-10: 1-932173-86-2
   ISBN-13: 978-1-932173-86-4
   Granny McFanny is so capable at everything she does, including
trapeze artist, fisherman, and being mayor of her town, that she
becomes president.

[1. Grandmothers–Fiction. 2. Success–Fiction.] I. Title. II. Polanco,
Jorge Bethancourt, ill.
[E]   2008
2008923620

STEPHENS PRESS, LLC
A Stephens Media Company

Post Office Box 1600
Las Vegas, NV 89125-1600
www.stephenspress.com

Printed in Hong Kong

Dedicated to Blake, Haley, and Ashley
for laughing and loving my bedtime tales.
And to my husband, Stefan, who faithfully offers me
support and endless encouragement to pursue my dreams.
–KAH

Granny McFanny threw a party
with balloons of blue and red.

Streamers flew around the room
and landed on her head.

Granny ate cake and cookies,
then clowns ran in the door.

They made her laugh so very hard
she fell onto the floor.

Granny McFanny joined the circus
and rode atop a giraffe.

She stopped and posed a moment
for a photograph.

6

Granny climbed a trapeze ladder
and flew above the crowd.

She flipped from one bar to another.
The crowd cheered very loud.

Granny McFanny went salsa dancing,
with a red rose in her hair.

8

She twirled across the dance floor
as others stopped to stare.

They shined the spotlight on her.
Granny really was a hit!

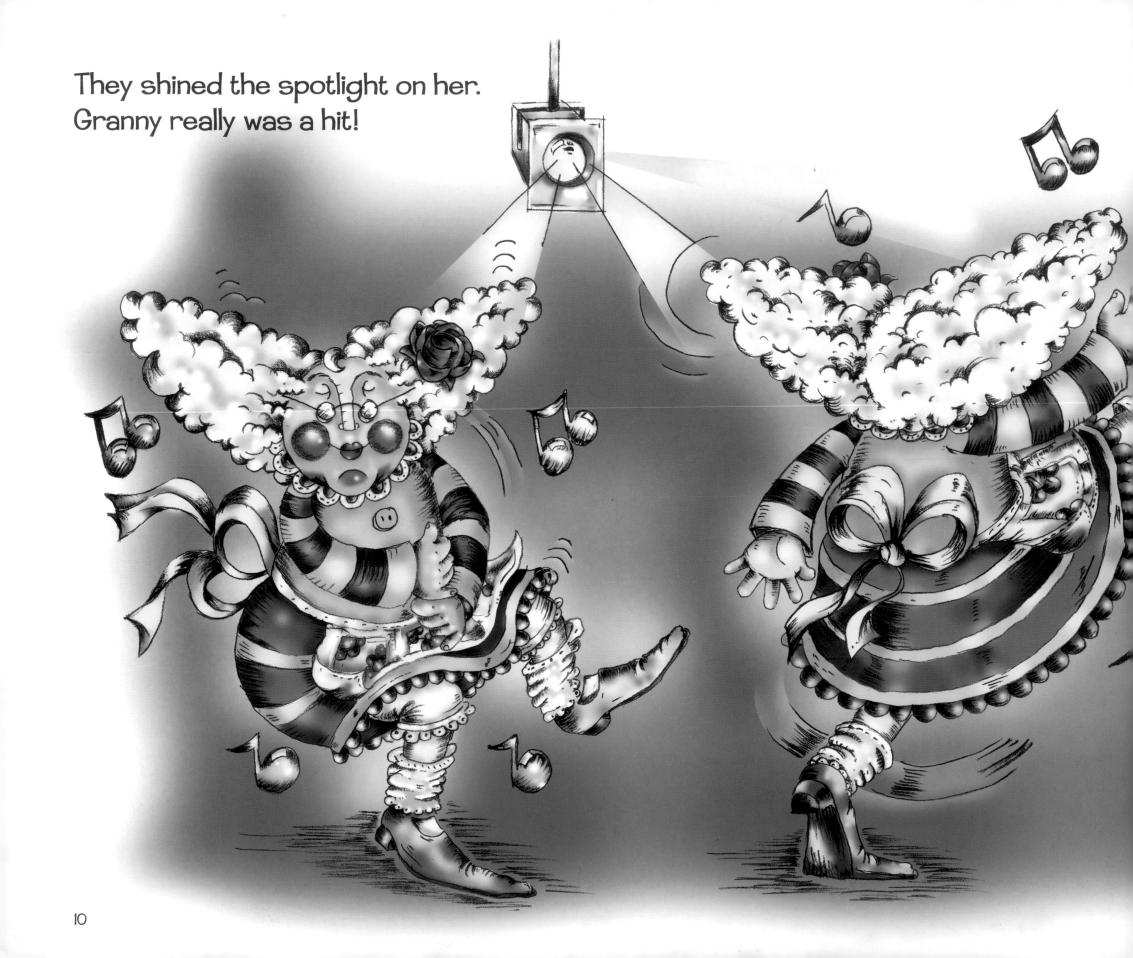

She spun around, lost her shoe
and landed in a split.

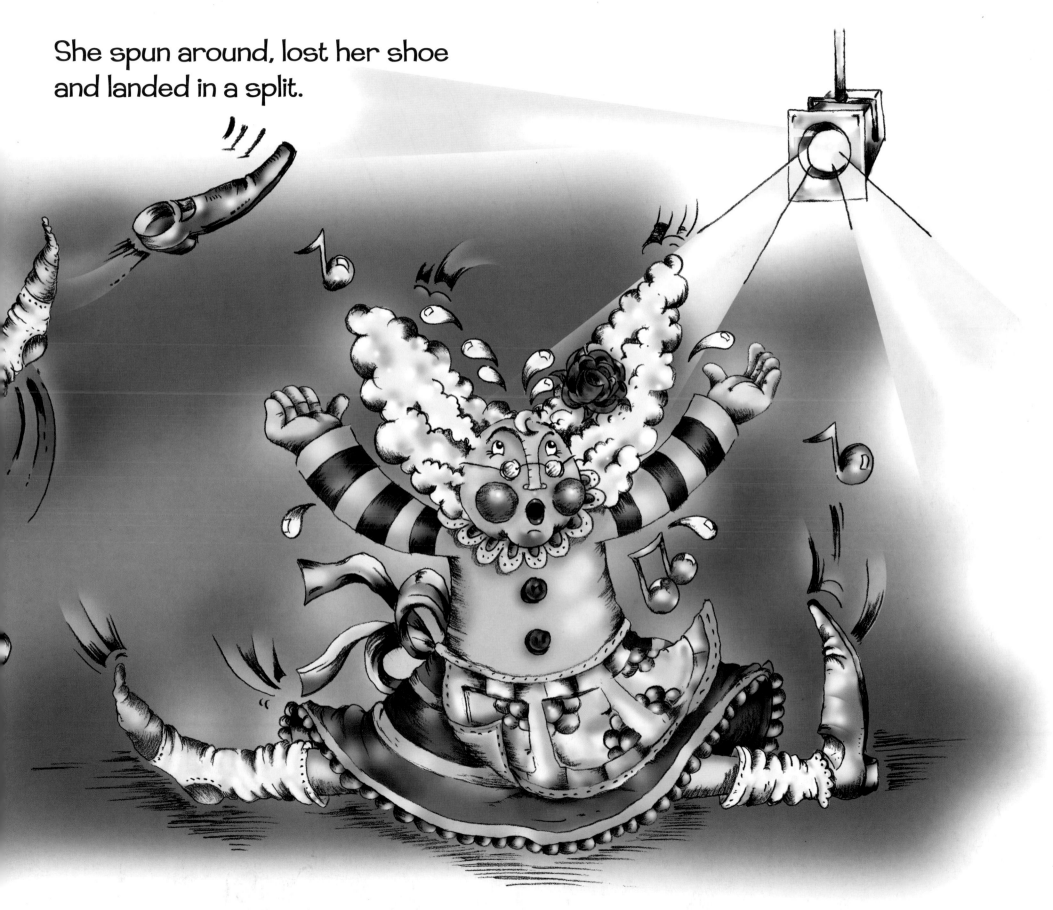

Granny McFanny went deep sea fishing on a boat with Captain Nick.

The waves went up and down so much it nearly made her sick.

Granny caught a great big fish,
but quickly set it free.

She threw the fish overboard
and it swam back out to sea.

Granny McFanny was a magician
and sawed a man in half.

A dove flew from her shiny cape.
The folks began to laugh.

Granny tried another trick,
and pulled a rabbit from her hat.

The bunny hopped around the stage
and into one man's lap.

Granny McFanny performed in the rodeo
upon a wild horse.

She got stuck in the saddle.
and galloped around the course.

The rodeo clowns tried to save her
and reached to grab her hands.

The horse kicked up so very high
it bucked her to the stands.

Granny McFanny went snow skiing
and glided down with grace.

When suddenly a snowball
hit her directly in the face.

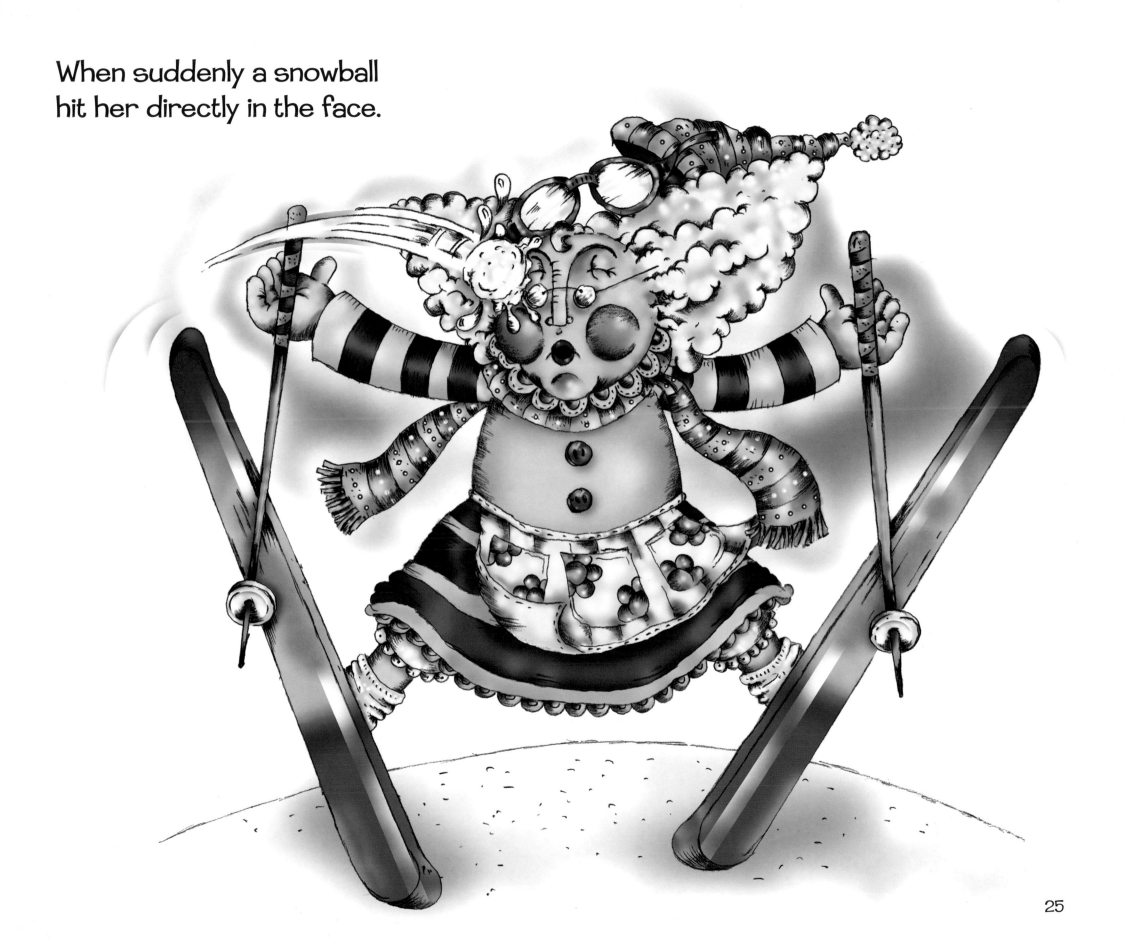

Granny weaved and wobbled
and then she lost a ski.

She tumbled down the mountain and landed in a tree.

Granny McFanny was elected Mayor.
She cleaned up the whole town.

She built parks and play centers
for kids from all around.

Granny made new friends
and spoke at every big event.

Granny McFanny did such a good job they made her president.